CLOSING COSTS

Closing Costs

Wesley Southard

For McKinney,
"Welcome to the house
of your dreams!"

Closing Costs © 2018 by Wesley Southard
Cover art and design © Whutta Design whutta.com
Layout design © Gypsy Press

All rights reserved. No portion of the book may be reproduced without written consent from the author.

This is a work of fiction. Names, characters, places and incidents are either a product of the author's imagination or are used fictitiously. Any resemblance to actual events, locals or persons living or dead, is entirely coincidental.

Author's Note: Although I have received technical assistance from a longtime professional in field, I have taken some fictional liberties with certain local laws involved in realty and the act of home buying/selling.

For Katie…
You…too…

Many thanks to Kelli Owen and Bob Ford, Mary SanGiovanni and Brian Keene, the No*Con crew, Mike Lombardo and Lex Quinn, and my wife, friends, and family for their love and encouragement. Extra special thanks to Ron Dickie for your eyes and laughs, to Steve Dossett for your technical help, and to Matt Hayward and Anna Hayward for your assistance with the dialogue.

"There is no place like home."
— Judy Garland

"Sometimes dead is better."
— Stephen King, *Pet Sematary*

ONE

He did not know their names, only that their severed limbs would not stop moving. Their fingers and bloodstained toes spasmed and clawed angrily in his direction, but the nails he had pounded into the floor kept them at bay. He hung his head. Tears spilled down his cheeks.

He had failed again.

It didn't matter how many times he tried, or how many different words he spoke or accents he used, it always ended the same way. Much like his very existence, the mess was blunt and plentiful—his machete and claw hammer saw to that—though he preferred to keep the disorder to a minimum. Noise wasn't necessarily an issue, not down here. Nor were the vagrants he used for his incantations. They wouldn't be missed.

The problem was he was running out of time.

A detached arm on the floor strained against its nail. Fingers scratched at the concrete, nails bending backwards and snapping, and the skin on its wrist widened and tore. Old, dark blood stained the floor beneath it. He carefully closed the old leather book, and then took the incensed gray hand in his own and squeezed gently.

"I'll get this right," he wept. "I'll get you better soon."

From across the room, a man's decapitated head moaned in the candlelight.

Wesley Southard

TWO

Monique Merkley was high-quality at a great many things. She was the first in her family to graduate high school, not to mention the first to finish all four years and graduate college, which she did handily with a communications and broadcasting degree from Indiana University. For the last fifteen years, she was the lead anchor for the local NBC affiliate, and was the first African American to do so in the Southern Indiana region. For the last six years, she had hosted a wildly popular, bipartisan podcast called *It's Up to You*, where she traveled the country, interviewing various politicians from city- to state-held positions, and impressively even a few ex-Presidents. She was highly regarded in her field, worked like hell to get there, and had a shelf full of local Emmys and various other prestigious awards to prove it. At forty-six, she still managed to turn heads and was regularly hit on when she was out around town. And every day she still managed to make her husband Hershel green with envy.

But at the moment he wasn't envious…just nervous. Underneath the blankets, Monique did her best to wake him from his late night studying and reviews. The blue-checkered comforter rose and fell, as did his chest as he sucked in deep, stuttering breaths. Twenty-three years of marriage and she still surprised him like this on mornings when she knew he really needed the pick-me-up.

Consider me picked up, he thought.

Her long brown curls exited the blanket, and she kissed him deeply. Morning breath filled each other's mouths. She grabbed both of his wrists and pressed them firmly against the mahogany headboard. Hershel grinned as she let him enter her. Slowly she rocked on top of him, the bed squeaking in her rhythm.

"You know you're going to do great today, right?"

Hershel could only nod. He had to concentrate. He looked away to the far wall, his eyes roaming the books on their joint shelf.

"Hey," she said. "Look at me."

…five, six, seven, eight books… he thought.

She grabbed his goateed chin, forcing him to lock eyes with her. "Hey! Eyes up here, old man. You can do this."

He nodded again. "Yes. Ok."

"Yes what?"

"Yes, Mrs. Merkley."

"That's better, old man." She bucked a little harder, grinding her hips into him. "You've got this. I believe in you."

Grunting, Hershel bit his lip and focused. Though her eyes were hypnotizing, her large breasts swung just above his face, obscuring his vision. Dark brown nipples gently swept across his cheeks. He moaned.

"Don't you dare," she growled in a loud whisper. "Just a little longer—I'm almost there!"

He shook his head, desperately trying to heed her words… though they were just words, and he was just as pathetic as he thought he would be. After a few moments, he broke her grasp and hugged her hips. He quivered, spilling himself within her. He stayed locked on for a few more gasps before falling backwards onto his pillow. He wanted to die. "I'm so sorry, hon."

She sighed and put her hands on his heaving chest. "It's ok."

"No…it's not. Maybe we can try again later?" He knew damn well at his age that would have been next to impossible. He wasn't a young man anymore.

"Maybe," she said, pulling herself off of him. She sat on

Closing Costs

the corner of the bed to put on her bra and panties. "But probably not. We've got the Hesston Banquet tonight, and we're going to be getting home fairly late."

"Try again tomorrow morning?"

She stood and put on her white cotton bathrobe. "It's a date." She winked, though half-heartedly, and left the room.

"Hey!" he called out.

Monique poked her head back in.

"I love you, Mrs. Merkley.

She grinned, "You too, old man," then left.

Fuming, Hershel slammed his head several times into his pillow, calling himself every terrible name he could think of. It was getting worse. Though Monique was as understanding as the day was long, he had lost patience with himself and his body long ago. It only worsened the older he got.

He dejectedly crawled out from bed and ambled onto the cold tiles of the bathroom floor. He switched on the shower and stared at himself hard in the mirror. Though he hated that he couldn't properly hold himself off for his wife, she did all but kill his nervousness about today's possible sale. He checked his chin and cheeks thoroughly in the mirror, content he would not have to shave around his goatee or lather up his slick baldhead. He checked his nose hairs, eyebrows, and inside his ears—all neat and trimmed. For his clients, he always wanted to look his best. A sloppy realtor meant sloppy investments, and he sure as hell couldn't afford to drop the ball on this one. Too much money at stake.

"You're a strong, intelligent, charming, smart, good-looking black man. You can sell this house. *Dobro pozhalovat' v dom vashey mechty.*" His reflection nodded back at him. He looked satisfied. Confident. "You've got this, old man."

He looked down at his groin accusingly. "You, on the other hand, *comrade*, have some serious work to do."

THREE

At the office, Hershel spent the early morning much like he did most. He got caught up on phone calls, texts, and anything he didn't get finished the day before. Paperwork was filed, inspections were ordered, and envelope after envelope was stuffed with various promotional items printed with his headshot and signature grin. He mailed dozens of free Otters baseball tickets for his various clients across the county, and he answered numerous emails from potential buyers. He enjoyed this time of the morning. It was nice and quiet, and it would still be another hour before most of the other realtors and the employees of the AAA they shared the building with would show up. George Benson and fresh mocha coffee permeated the air of his cubical.

"*Dobro pozhalovat' v dom vashey mechty. Dobro pozhalovat' v dom vashey mechty.*" He repeated the simple Russian phrase like a mantra. He was reasonably confident he had it down.

Once finished with menial tasks, he opened up the company's website to once again refresh himself with the property before heading off to meet his only clients of the day. And what a pair they were. Evgeni Sokolov and his wife Yana. Though the name meant virtually nothing to him, if he were to ask someone half his age he was sure they would have brightened significantly. Most of his peers liked to study up on their clients before meeting face to face, but Hershel preferred going in mostly dry of information. He was naturally a people person, and if there was one thing most people liked to do, they enjoyed talking about themselves, especially those with money. It put them at ease, helped them to loosen up. He figured knowing that Mr. Sokolov had enough money to fly to Southwestern Indiana just to look at the Whitecomb mansion, they would have plenty to talk about. He only knew the man was a music producer in Los Angeles, mainly in the hip hop and pop genre, which is why the name didn't ring a bell. He knew nothing of the man's wife either.

What surprised him the most was they had inquired about *him* specifically, and he didn't know why. Though he had been a certified realtor for nearly eighteen years, he wasn't even the most qualified to sell a home of this magnitude. One of nearly twenty in his office, Hershel was at his best selling starter homes to young people fresh from college, or married couples looking to upgrade to a quiet cul-de-sac in the suburbs. Most of his peers didn't like dealing with the twenty-year-olds, but he didn't mind. He quite enjoyed helping them find their first place to call their own outside of their parents' or a dorm room. The commissions weren't great, but their hopeful smiles gave him more than money could.

But today? Today could finally put him over the top.

He just hoped Colin Whitecomb would stay out of his way.

The front glass door swung open, and Bryan Dossett strolled leisurely into the office, singing along with his oversized Beats by Dre headphones. Hershel cringed and turned down his radio. *Every. Single. Morning.*

"*Yoooouuuu! You got what I neeeeeed! But you say you're just a friend! But you say you're just a friend—oh, baby, yooouu…*"

Hershel waved as he walked passed.

"Hey, big Hersh, my man! What's happening, brother?" He took off his headphones and slapped Hershel's open palm with gusto. Typically he hated when white folks unnecessarily 'blacked up' their conversation with him. It happened occasionally with clients, but not often. Dossett was one of his oldest friends in the business, had even trained him when he started with Owen and Ford Realty, and he had always talked to Hershel a little bolder than most would. With him,

Closing Costs

he didn't mind it too much. He meant no disrespect.

"Good morning, Bryan."

Dossett placed his briefcase in the cubical across the aisle. "You're in awful early, eh. And quite spiffy-looking, I might add. Nervous about today?"

Hershel grinned at the South Dakota accent Dossett was still trying to hide. "A little, I guess. Trying not to think about it."

"A little, my ass. I've sold some big houses, Hersh, but the Whitecomb place? Yowza! We've been trying to sell that place for how long now? Hell, I've thrown my hat into that, what, three times now, and zilch. I'd have an easier time selling a birthday cake to a diabetic than getting that place off our hands."

"Well, it's not exactly like Warrick and Vanderburgh Counties are dripping with multi-millionaires looking to over-upgrade."

Dossett clapped. "And that, big Hersh, is why I'm jealous as hell those russkies asked for you to be their man."

Hershel turned to face him. "Come on, Dossett. No need for the ethnic slurs."

"You're right, you're right," Dossett said with his hands held up. "I'm sure they're just perfectly nice Russians looking for a house in Newburgh, Indiana instead of New York or LA or literally anywhere else that would make sense for a couple of filthy rich moguls."

"I'm sorry, you moved to Indiana by choice, did you not?"

Dossett laughed, "Have you ever been to South Dakota? Much like Russia we don't get much sunlight, fashion is fifteen years behind, and it snows nine months out of the year. At least there are seasons here."

"And that can be a big selling point."

Groaning, Dossett collapsed into his desk chair. He

rubbed his tired eyes. "I'm just saying it's a little weird that two people with no ties to the area are looking to drop a mint on that place."

"Is that a hint of jealously I detect?"

"Fuck yeah, it's jealously! The commission alone would be able to afford me that Challenger I've had my eye on for the last three years. Orange with black racing stripes." He whistled. "But I am happy you're getting this, Hersh. This is going to put you over the top with your vacation fund, right?"

Hershel nodded. *Bingo.*

He rarely kept secrets from his wife; he had no reason to. Twenty-three years of marriage, and he still felt guilty when he lied about going to Hooters with the guys for wings and to watch the Colts games. *But this secret?* He'd been keeping this one since the day he started with Owen and Ford.

"The Caribbean, right?" Dossett asked.

"No. The Maldives." For eighteen years, only about seventy-five percent of his commissions made it to their joint bank account. The rest he hid in a separate account in a credit union across town, and he never spoke a word about it. It was only about a month ago after being contacted by the Sokolov's did he realize just how close he was to hitting his ultimate goal. A quick tallying up, and the commission from the Whitecomb sale would finally put him over. He was thrilled he was finally going to be able to give Monique the honeymoon she never got all those years ago.

"Isn't that the place where you stay in those little cabanas right over the water? Basically an island, right?"

"Yes," Hershel answered. "Look it up. It's unbelievable. Mo's been talking about that place since we were first dating. It's extraordinarily expensive, but if I can make this sale today then I can finally take her on the trip of her dreams. I'll have enough funds to rent out a cabana for an entire month. I'm going to surprise her tonight at the Hesston Banquet."

"If you make the sale."

Hershel sighed. "If I make the sale."

"And if you don't? Then how long before you can do it?"

"If not…maybe seven, eight more years."

Dossett whistled nervously. "Well then, big Hersh, you better not fuck it up. Before you know it you'll be too old make a twenty hour flight, and your saggy ball bag will be hitting the ocean water before your feet do."

Grinning, Hershel nodded. "That, we can agree on."

"You've got to be dreading it though, right? Having to tell them about the murder?"

Hershel closed his eyes and grimaced.

FOUR

Immense pain blossomed in both of her legs, waking Tara from a deep sleep she didn't know she was in. She sucked in a harsh, unsettling breath and began to cry again. Tara was sick of crying. Everything hurt now, even crying. It seemed as though all she did now was sleep, but what else could she do when everything was just so cold and off-white. The doctors and nurses were just as frigid. Nurse Scofield was nice to her though. She gave her ice cream.

She tried to sit up, but her lower back throbbed as bad as her legs. She wasn't sure she had any tears left, but they poured down her reddened cheeks hot and steady. Her pillow dampened around her neck. Shaking, she reached for the button to call the nurses, but she couldn't find it. It must have fallen off the bed again. This brought more tears.

The room was dark, and the even beeps of her heart monitor were a constant reminder of just how alone she was. Other than doctors and nurses, no one came to visit her. Not even her daddy. She hadn't seen him in so long. Desperately she wanted him to hold her hand, to hug her, kiss her cheek and help her fight the Lukey that made everything hurt so much. *That's what it's called*, she thought. *Lukey. Or Lukey-mia or something.* Either way she needed help.

She tried to sit up once more, to look past the white curtain to outside of her room, but the door was only slightly cracked open. Even if she could manage to yell, which judging by her difficulty swallowing, she didn't believe she could be loud enough for anyone to hear. Carefully Tara allowed herself to drop backwards. She closed her red-hot eyes to rest once more, not knowing when another bout of pain would hit.

FIVE

Psychologically impacted property.

Hershel repeated the words over and over as he drove down the Lloyd Expressway into Newburgh. He hated the term. Despised it even. Though not many, it cost him sales in the past. And it was the reason why the Whitecomb mansion was still on the market after nine long years.

He drove in silence, a raw, acidic taste building in his throat. He popped a strawberry mint into his mouth, but he began to chew it instead of letting it naturally dissolve. Up until this point he had been cool and calm. He shouldn't be nervous, he had no reason to be. He was good at his job—damn good. He was friendly, personable even when faced with less than ideal clients, and he knew his shit. Which is exactly why he was now dreading his legal obligation to disclose what happened all those years ago.

He remembered the night Monique broke the news on her show. It chilled him then, and it chilled him now. Harris Whitecomb, local sheet rock spreader turned Mega Millions lottery winner, went to sleep the night of July 18th in his king sized bed inside his multi-million dollar home and was found the next morning a little lighter above the shoulders. He had been decapitated in his sleep by his sixteen-year-old son Cameron. It was Cameron's twin brother Colin who had found their father, *sans* head, early the next morning. After a few hours, it reached national news, but it had quickly dissipated once something of more importance arose. For weeks, the police searched for Cameron Whitecomb. No one, not even Colin, knew where he had disappeared to. He left all his belongings, took no money, and left no motives behind. The police were at a stalemate. Colin, being too young to have claim to the home and having no relatives to look after him, was given up to the state until he was eighteen. The rest of Harris Whitecomb's lottery winnings, which was said to be in the tens of millions, was never found. Mr. Whitecomb never divulged where he held his money, and the whereabouts of his earnest fortune disappeared with several strikes of a half-sharpened machete.

That's why the house remained empty and caked in filthy layers of undesirable lore. Nine years and every potential sale ended in a curt "Thanks, but no thanks." No one could sell it. Hershel planned on changing that today. He had to.

After taking a left onto Bell Road, he turned right onto Oak Grove and drove until the houses and subdivisions dissolved into hills, stripper pits, and dead, yellowed cornfields. It hadn't snowed in the last few weeks, and he hoped that the maintenance company they had hired to keep the property cleaned up had done the job they were paid handsomely for. By the time he pulled up to the long paved driveway, he was happy to see they had.

The cool March air bit him as he stepped out of his car. He shivered and pulled the collar of his suit jacket up higher around his neck. Though he normally wore a polo and slacks to his appointments, today he wanted to look his absolute best, so he went to Men's Warehouse and purchased a reasonably pricey suit to match the house. He didn't wear suits often, but he liked how it made him feel. Quickly, he checked himself in the reflection of the car window, satisfied. He turned to the massive home and sneered. *You're not beating me today.*

Behind him, a slick red Lexus convertible purred into the driveway. It pulled to a stop behind his Honda CRV, and the man he only knew from pictures on the Internet exited the car. Evgeni Sokolov appeared much shorter than Hershel had anticipated, though to be fair, at six foot four most people were smaller than him. The man couldn't have

Closing Costs

been much bigger than five-five, and probably weighted less than an empty shopping cart. Posh was the word that came to mind when Hershel looked over the Russian's outfit: slick Italian loafers, a purple Gucci t-shirt with kakis, and brand new Burberry round-framed sunglasses. The only thing he wouldn't call posh was his childlike bowl haircut that stopped just above his eye line, though he wore it with confidence, so Hershel couldn't knock him for that.

Hershel smiled and held his hands up high. "*Dobro pozhalovat' v dom vashey mechty!*"

"Ha ha!" the Russian laughed, clapping. "'Welcome to the house of your dreams!' I like it! You've been practicing your Russian, *da?*"

"That I have, Mr. Sokolov."

The man approached Hershel and he was somehow even smaller than he was standing by his car. They shook hands. "No no with formalities. Please, call me Geno. That is my professional name. Is what the kids know me by?" Though his accent was thick, Hershel had no problem understanding him.

"Well then, Geno, I'm Hershel Merkley. Welcome to Indiana. I trust you had no problem finding the place?"

"No problem. Rental car has...how you say...GPS? Is very nice car. Many bells and whistles."

"How was your flight from LA?"

"Was not bad. We had layover in Atlanta, but we get here quickly." He turned to face the house, which towered over them both. "Is big home, no? *Ochen' bol'shoy.* Everything in America big. I like what I see, my friend." He winked at Hershel.

Hershel wasn't sure what he meant, but he shook it off. "So did you come alone?"

"No no. Yana is in car. She no like the cold. You would think Russian woman would like cold, but she no like it.

Sometimes I think she is Finnish." He whistled toward the car.

Yana Sokolov didn't exactly step out of the car—she slithered out of it. She rose from the passenger side door and glided toward him with the ease and grace of a runway model, her large four-inch heels lightly clicking the pavement. She was nearly a whole head taller than her husband, who quickly wrapped his arm around her waist as she came forward. Long straw colored hair cascaded over her shoulders, and though she had spent the day flying across the country, her thick pouty lips were perfectly concealed in hot pink lipstick. Her almond shaped hazel eyes looked him up and down.

Hershel put out his hand, which she lightly accepted. "How was your flight, Mrs. Sokolov?"

She didn't answer, only looked toward her much smaller husband. Evgeni said, "Don't be offended, Hershel. Unlike me, she speak very little English. She is fashion model in LA. She only know words like 'Turn', 'Change', and 'Hungry'. I try to teach more words, but she stubborn like Ox." He turned to her. "Yana, do like what you see? *Nu kak tebe? Nravitsya?*"

She smiled. "*Da.*"

"Excellent!" Geno said. "Then we move inside now. We have much to see, much to discuss, my friend."

Hershel said, "Absolutely," and led them up the pristinely edged walkway to the front door. His nerves were all but gone. He smiled to himself, knowing he could pull this off. He reached for the Ebox. His fingers lightly brushed the doorknob.

The door was already open.

Hershel's smile faded. He didn't believe the groundskeepers had any access to the inside of the house, but maybe they had been in to use the bathrooms. Maybe one his coworkers didn't properly lock up the last time they were here. Either way, he didn't like it. He stared at the crack in the door and clicked his tongue.

"Is problem?" Geno asked.

Hershel shook his head. "Nope. No problem at all." He carefully grabbed the doorknob and closed it, then after punching in the key code he took the key from the Ebox and pretended to unlock the door. *All about appearances*, he thought. He pushed the door open and stepped aside to let them though. When they entered the house, Hershel quickly stepped back outside and glanced around. Though he had no idea who opened the house, he knew damn well who could have. He lived just down the hill. And he prayed he wouldn't be a roadblock today.

SIX

He grunted as he ripped the machete from the homeless woman's skull. Several red-stained teeth and a long strip of wet skin flew in his recoil. The teeth clattered about the numerous other body parts already littered across the floor. From the other side of the room, anchored limbs continued their futile scratching for their unmaker. The salt enclosing them remained untouched.

The woman grunted as she toppled backwards, though she had no arms or legs to brace herself. Blood squelched across the dusty concrete but never broke the salt circle. The droplets that did hit the small white granules popped and sizzled. He dropped to a knee, tired and more defeated than ever. His machete dripped warm red onto the floor.

The woman lifted her head and grinned, the deep gash in her skull opening wider. "You fail, human." Her voice gurgled like water going down a drain.

Baring his teeth, the man growled, "What am I doing wrong, damn you! Why won't you tell me?"

Raw, broken skin began to slide backwards from her face. "You do not listen well, human. You cry like a wounded animal. And much like animals you do not listen to my words." Wisps of gray smoke leaked from her mouth.

The man screamed, "*Tell me!*"

"Six eyes, three souls. You do not bring this to me. Over and over you bring two and one. You want to speak to him? You want your answers? You do as I request."

"I don't understand!" he said, frustrated. "'Six eyes, three souls'? What the fuck does that even mean?"

Her ruined cranium continued to split and widen. A small blue tentacle wormed out of the hole in the woman's face, pushing the ruined yolk of her eye from its socket. "I will not repeat myself, human. You have but one more attempt. If you fail, I will take *your* two and one with me, and you can visit your father for the rest of eternity. You will burn right along with him, be one with the infinite fire. I will personally oversee your eternal torment. It would be my divine pleasure."

Cameron Whitecomb stood and backed away as the tentacle elongated and stretched across the woman's face until it reached her chest. Its mucusy skin slowly dragged across the homeless woman's breasts and nipples. Her skull cracked wider, and her smile grew with it.

Witnesses, he thought anxiously. *It requires witnesses.*

Just above him, the front door creaked open, and multiple pairs of footsteps walked across the upstairs floor.

SEVEN

The interior of the house wasn't quite as warm as he would have liked, but Hershel had to imagine it would cost a small fortune to keep the place warm. A small fortune he hoped the Sokolovs planned on dropping today. He ushered them into the foyer before closing the wide, double set front doors behind them.

His cell phone buzzed in his pocket.

"My apologies, Geno," Hershel said, embarrassed. "I usually have my cell turned to silent when I'm with clients."

Evgeni waved him off, glancing around at the high vaulted ceilings of the entryway and the shimmering chandelier that hung high over their heads. "Is no problem. Please, take call. You are busy man, no?"

Hershel checked his caller ID and saw it was Monique. He held a finger up to his client and stepped away toward the staircase on his left that led down to the half-finished basement. He answered, "Hello, Mrs. Merkley."

"Hello, yourself, old man," his wife cooed. "How's it going?"

"We just got here. We're inside the house."

"Oh, shoot! I'm sorry. I didn't mean to interrupt. I'll let you go."

"No, hey," he stopped her. "It's fine. I've got a minute. Is everything alright?"

"Yes, everything's perfect. How are the Russians?"

He turned to glance as the irregularly sized couple slowly walked about the room, Yana and her clicking heels staying at arm's length to her husband. They quietly spoke to one another, though he couldn't make out the words. Unfortunately he had only practiced one phrase in their language. "They're maybe a little jetlagged, but fine. The wife doesn't speak much English, so the husband Geno does all the talking. They seem nice though."

"Geno, huh? You're already on a first name basis?"

"For the moment, yes…until I have to tell them about you know what."

"I understand," she said. "So do you feel nervous? Do you think you can make the sale?"

Hershel grinned. "I think so."

"Yeah?" he heard her grin too.

"You bet."

"Ok, old man, well I'll let you get back to it. Oh—before I let you go. Don't forget about the Hesston Banquet tonight. Seven o'clock. Please don't be late." Monique had the distinct privilege to host a special event the Old National Events Plaza later that evening. Live on stage, she would be conducting an exclusive interview with local celebrity Lydia Hesston, a deep space astronaut, who the Mayor of Evansville wanted to honor for her contributions to the community and the world at large. Hershel himself would have been nervous as hell in front of hundreds of the most wealthy and powerful people in the area, but Monique spoke to most of them through her show on a nightly basis. She had been prepping for weeks and was more than prepared to shine.

Hershel checked his watch. Ten after twelve. "We'll be done way before then. Plenty of time to clean up and get ready."

"Sounds good. I'll see you tonight."

"One more thing."

"Yes?" she asked.

He hesitated. "I may have a surprise for you tonight."

"Oh yeah?"

"We shall see. Ok, got to go."

"Good bye, old man." She hung up.

Closing Costs

Hershel placed the phone back in his pocket and sighed. The pressure was on now. He turned to face his wandering clients. "Sorry about that. My wife wanted to remind me of something we had planned for this evening. Now where were we?"

Yana Sokolov visibly frowned, but it was quickly replaced with a tight-lipped smile.

"Is no problem, Hershel," Evgeni said. "Wives always there to remind us of things we may forget. What is wife's name, may I ask?"

"Monique."

"Monique? I like that. Is very American name. Is she beautiful like Yana?"

Hershel was taken aback by the callowish question. He wasn't sure what to say. He quickly answered, "Very much so, yes."

Yana blushed and turned away.

"Yana is very beautiful, and I would have it no other way," Evgeni boasted. "Is how we met, you know? She wanted to be singer in Russia, but she not sing very well. She have long legs and pretty face, but no harmony. Is shame, no? She make money now as model, but with me she could have been huge singer."

"I've been meaning to ask you, Geno, what is it you do exactly?" Hershel led them through the entryway into a short hallway off to their right and into the first of three living areas on the main floor. The glass sunroof overhead bled midday sun across the mocha colored walls and the pristinely maintained white trim floorboards. Beautiful paintings, rich velvet couches and chairs accented the high arched windows and dark wooden floors, giving the room an almost 'too lofty to be lounged in' vibe. The type only to be admired.

Evgeni straightened the collar on his shirt, visibly happy to finally talk about himself. "Little old me?" he joked. "I am record producer in Los Angeles, California. I help make music for the kids to dance to. I am originally from Yaroslavl, Russia. Much bigger than this place, but much smaller than Los Angeles. I used to make…what do you call it…house music. Music for disco. People dance, use drugs, have fun. But it make me no money. Not much money in Russia. None for music. So I save money and move to California to make music in America. Music make more money here." After quickly eyeing the room, he slowly left and walked back into the hallway, Yana following. Hershel kept up behind them. It was best to give the client space to breathe, let them get their own feel of the place without rushing them through.

They entered the kitchen, and Evgeni leisurely strolled around the room. He ran his fingers across the large, granite-topped island in the middle of the floor. "The big problem is no one heard of Evgeni Sokolov in America. Maybe I was big deal in snowy Russia, but in sunny America I was nobody. I had to make myself a somebody." He eyed the stainless steel appliances and custom cabinetry throughout the open kitchen. Yana stayed near the fridge, checking her cell phone. "Have you ever heard of Megan Masters?"

Hershel shook his head. "No, I don't believe so."

"You should," Evgeni said. "She not my favorite, but she can sing. She new pop singer. Record company was struggling to find young girl a hit song. I brought them song I had made, and they loved it. Have you heard 'Whisper in the Castle'?"

"Maybe," Hershel lied. "I'm not sure."

He sang, "'Whisper in the castle, hold me close and don't let go! Screaming just to hear me, you hold the key to my soul!'"

Hershel laughed. "Yes, I believe I have heard that somewhere."

"Of course you have. It big hit all over the world. I did that. Those my words, my music. It may have made her big star, but I make big money. Suddenly Geno in demand. It Geno this, Geno that. Everybody want a little Geno on their albums. It make me very wealthy man. We no longer live in apartment. We own very big home in Los Angeles. We also own condo in New York City. I get everything I want now."

Internally, Hershel cringed. He'd been around some high rollers, but Geno certainly took the full-of-shit cake. "Well, congratulations on all your success. It sounds like you've found your piece of the American dream."

Evgeni nodded, already walking out of the room past Hershel. "*Da.* American Pie and all that."

They walked past yet another living area, this one with crimson colored walls and double sliding doors that led to the back patio and pool area. Beyond the fenced-in yard were miles of corn stalks, yellowed and long dead from winter. Evgeni briefly stopped in the dining room, only to carefully tap his foot on the handsome decorative rug beneath the dining table.

Hershel turned to find Yana standing a few steps behind. Her eyes met his, and her thick, pouting lips curled into a smile. Hershel gave her a professional smile back and a nod and turned away. He was afraid he would stare too long. Though he couldn't be sure, he was fairly certain he had never been around a model before, much less someone who used their looks for a living. She was quite striking, gorgeous even, but not quite his type. He'd been with plenty of beautiful women in his youth, when his stomach was still flat and his head still had hair, but he doubted that even at his peak he would have been able to land a woman like Yana. It didn't bother him much though. The past was the past, and if everything went right today, he could spend a whole month with his wife in the middle of the Indian Ocean, soaking up the sun and making memories. And trying to fix his little problem.

"I have to ask," Hershel said. "If you've got all these homes around the country…why buy one here? I realize that may not be the best question to ask someone while trying to sell them a home, but I've been curious since first hearing from you. Why not someplace like Nashville or Chicago, or even Atlanta?"

Evgeni quickly checked out one of the two half baths on the main floor before closing the door and walking away. Hershel noticed how aloof he seemed in his discoveries. "I like those places, but they very loud and noisy, much like other two homes. Musicians easily distracted. When they have mind on something else, they no make good music. We look into house here so that I may build big studio in basement, and we can be away from discos and parties. Artists need focus. This place seems like it far enough away from big lights and…how do you say…culture? *Da*, culture. It boring here. No culture, no nightlife. Nothing to do. Artist will only want to work, not play."

Though it made perfect sense to Hershel, he felt like he should have been offended. But the more he thought about it, unfortunately, he might have been right. Nowhere to go in a two-hour radius.

"Well, Geno, I'm happy you chose to come here to the Tri-State and check in on our house and everything we have to offer here. It sounds as though you have it all figured out. Though I have to say, we have lots of things to do here locally. We have professional baseball and ice hockey teams, as well as college basketball if you're into sports. Plenty of great restaurants in Evansville and Newburgh, and several venues to see concerts and shows. They've been revitalizing downtown for the last few years, so it's steadily growing and improving. It's small, but there's plenty to offer."

"And corn," Evgeni said. "Corn fields everywhere. I get off plane and I see corn. Why so much corn?"

"It has to come from somewhere, right?"

Closing Costs

"Very strange. It go in whole, it come out whole. I don't like it."

Laughing, Hershel led them back to the main entryway. They passed a service elevator, which Evgeni pointed to and gave a thumbs-up. "I like this. Very nice."

"So," Hershel inquired. "What are your thoughts so far, Geno? Is it everything you and your lovely wife hoped for?"

Evgeni nodded solemnly. He appeared disinterested in continuing their introductory tour. "*Da.* Is very good. Very big. Not as big as other house, but very big."

Something warmed in Hershel's chest. "Well, I'm sure you've already seen the website, but I can go over the basics as listed here on the MLS sheet so you can know what kind of home this is—and that's what I want you to think of it as: a home. The more you think of it as a home, you start to see it as *your* home. That's what I'm trying to sell you: a new home. A new adventure. A new experience in your lives." Much like Monique, he'd been practicing his speech for a while, but unlike hers his was coming out a bit corny. He decided to scrap it. "Built in two thousand four, this home only had one previous owner before becoming available to you. We're nestled on two point six four acres of land, and we're currently standing in eleven thousand, six hundred and..." he checked his papers, "forty square feet of interior property. This home contains no less than five bedrooms and five full- and three half-bathrooms. Below our feet we have a half-finished basement with enough square footage to build your perfect recording studio. Outside, beyond the beautiful stone and stucco exterior, there's a fully enclosed backyard—with a privacy fence—that includes an in-ground heated pool and a hot tub. There's also a four car attached garage and a driveway big enough to park eight more. Back inside we have a twelve seated theater room with a ten foot projection screen. That elevator we passed travels from the basement to the second floor above us, for ease of access to every level. We've seen the kitchen, which features granite countertops, custom cabinetry, and a walk-in pantry. Upstairs we have a master suite with over a thousand square feet of space, gorgeous bamboo flooring, and its own private bath with a whirlpool and double vanities. Have I mentioned an abundance of closet space?"

He noticed Evgeni was not paying the slightest bit of attention to what he was saying. Back and forth, he and his wife made gestures as if urging the other one to say something. Neither one would budge.

"Is there something the matter?" Hershel asked.

Evgeni sighed. "No, there is no problem at all. Everything peachy."

"Well then, how about we go have a look at the upstairs, and I can show that incredible master suite. It's truly amazing to see. Practically a ballroom."

"In time," said the Russian. "How about I send Yana upstairs to look around, and we can have a little privacy to… discuss matters."

"Absolutely. No problem."

"Good." Evgeni turned to his wife. "*Yana, idi naverkh, pozhaluysta, mi poka obsudim nash vopros.*"

Yana said, "*Tolko ne isporti vse. Ya ego khochu.*"

"*Naverkh poshla, zhivo!*" he growled.

Nodding, Yana turned to give a quick look at Hershel before gracefully ascending the staircase. He watched her perfectly round rear end as it reached the top of the landing. Something stirred in Hershel's loins, but he quickly pushed it away. *Quit staring*, he thought nervously.

"Women," Evgeni said. "What is that saying? Can't live with them, can't leave them in cornfield for dogs."

Hershel grinned. "Something like that."

"Anyway, let us get back to business now that woman is not around."

"Absolutely. While she's perusing the upstairs, would you like to take a look at the basement, maybe get a feel for your potential studio space?"

Evgeni shook his head and wagged his finger. "No no. There is no need. I want house."

A tingling started in his toes and quickly spread throughout his body. His heart fluttered. Hershel nearly screamed with excitement. He did it. He finally did it.

"Wow!" he said. "Mr. Sokolov—I mean Geno! You haven't even seen the rest of the house yet."

"You mean home, *da*?"

Hershel laughed, maybe a bit too erratically. "Yes! Home—your home. I mean, don't you want to see the rest of the place? Honestly, we barely even covered the main floor. There's still much more to look over. I haven't even given you the asking price yet."

"Not necessary. I already see enough. I like home. Yana like home. We see pictures on website. We are satisfied. Money is no problem. We take it."

After years of futility by dozens of his peers, he finally succeeded where they had failed. He'd never been much of an athlete growing up, nor was he much into sports in general, but he imagined this was what it felt like to win a championship. He had never hugged a client, but he wanted to lift Evgeni Sokolov off the Italian marble floor and spin the tiny man like a prom date.

"Geno…" he stuttered. "I can't tell you how happy I am for you and your lovely wife. I think making this amazing place your home is just the right decision for you both."

"*Da*. I agree. But I have one thing I must ask of you before we call this deal, no?"

"Absolutely anything, Geno. You name it."

Evgeni put his hand on Hershel's shoulder and squeezed. "You must fuck my wife."

EIGHT

Yana looked down with a wry grin on her husband and the tall drink of water standing next to him. Evgeni spoke to him in hushed tones, or maybe she was out of hearing range, but she couldn't hear their words. Either way she knew exactly what they were discussing.

He better not screw this up for me, she thought.

She could still feel his eyes roaming her ass as she sashayed up the staircase, and even before when they first pulled up to the house. Though his suit was cheap, much like this shitty little hick town, he was everything she hoped for. That clean, baldhead, and his deep, sexy voice she could feel in her chest. Tall and lean, she wanted to climb him like a tree. Skin so smooth and brown his name should have been Hershey.

From down below, the realtor turned his head toward her, and she quickly hid out of sight.

Pressing herself against the wall, she hiked her dress up to her waist and pressed her first two fingers against her already damp panties. She moaned, though quietly, as she rubbed herself. She imagined what his big strong hands would feel like going up and down her body, and around her throat. She wanted him to be rough with her, wanted him to throw her around, slap her, bite her, and call her all those filthy things only American men knew how to say. More than anything she wanted Evgeni to watch.

She'd been that way for as long as she could remember. Even before becoming Mrs. Sokolov, Yana Petrov enjoyed being watched. Back in her home county, when she was in her teens, boyfriends would look on as many men would take her at once. It was the only thing that brought her to climax. One or a dozen, she didn't care how many had their way with her body, so long as others reveled. It wasn't about humiliation. She loved her boyfriends and past fiancés dearly, even now her husband, but she loved their eyes more than their touch. She wanted their desire, craved it. She wanted their undivided attention. If they chose to touch themselves, that was fine by her too.

By the time she reached America, her tastes had grown. She wanted more than the pretty men she modeled with. Most were gay, and those that were not had little interest in being part of her voyeurism. They were children, anyway. Little boys in fancy suits. She wanted real men. Everyday men. Men who lusted for her the way Evgeni did. She'd been with men of all colors and races, but when they found Hershel Merkley's picture on the realtor website, she suddenly got a taste for chocolate.

Yana didn't know how long she was standing there before she heard the soft *ding* of the elevator. Quickly, she dropped her dress and composed herself, expecting Hershel and her husband to walk around the corner wearing big, bright grins. She smoothed her hair and waited for them, her body a tingling hive of eagerness. When they never came, she rounded the corner just as the elevator door was closing. Beyond the door, the cab was empty.

That's weird, she thought. Maybe they went to another room…maybe they were waiting in the master bedroom. The thought made her sizzle with glee. Even if that were the case, she would make them wait for just a bit longer. Anticipation makes the heart grow fonder…and the panties grow wetter. She smiled.

In the next hallway she found four more doors, all closed except for one. The first door revealed a fairly large bedroom with a single queen sized bed sitting dead center in the room. She noted the size and wondered what she could use the room for. Exercise room, perhaps. Maybe a spa or massage room. She closed the door and opened the one directly across the hall. Another bathroom, full-sized this time, complete with wall length mirror and a shell-shaped washbasin. A little tacky for her tastes, but it would do, she supposed. The tub was impressive, but she was itching to see how big the one in the master suite was. She approached the final door at the end of the hall, and being already ajar, she pushed it the rest of the way open.

It is *like a ballroom*, she thought happily. Though she would have rather seen Hershel waiting for her on the king sized bed, the room itself was enough to keep her interest. Amber curtains hung over the numerous windows that faced out over the pool and backyard, with a wraparound balcony to look down on their guests. She didn't even bother with turning on the overhead chandelier, as the natural sunlight gorgeously illuminated the light bamboo flooring. Her clicking heels echoed off the walls. The noise that could be made in this room…

She stepped into the bathroom, and this time she clicked on the lights. Just as the website had described it. The whirlpool was delectable, as was the sizable shower just across from it. Both could fit numerous people at once. Though she preferred their master bath back in Los Angeles, this was nothing to sniff at.

Near the back of the room was the walk-in closet. *This* she wanted to see. She doubted it would have the optimal space to hold all of her designer clothes, but maybe it could hold her shoes. At this point she wasn't even sure how much time would be spent in this house, beyond her occasional visit while Evgeni worked.

She pulled open the door. The interior was pitch black. She went to flip the light switch, but she clammed up.

Near the back of the closet, something slowly stood. She gasped.

The darkness reached for her.

NINE

Maybe he misheard him. Words were very obviously lost in translation. Evgeni conversed in English well enough, but there was no way in hell he had meant to say that. Certainly he hadn't spoken correctly.

"Excuse me?" Hershel asked, flabbergasted.

"Fuck my wife," the Russian repeated. "I want you to fuck my wife."

Again, Hershel was very certain he was hearing him all wrong. He cocked his head, letting the man's brash words fill the air like a cancerous smog. He kept calm, and he spoke clear and concise. "Geno, I don't think you know what you're saying. Maybe we need to just move on and continue with what we were discussing before, yes?"

Evgeni raised his eyebrows, now looking like the one confused. "What is not to understand? I want house, you fuck my wife. Is simple."

Hershel sighed, his frustration building. "Listen, Geno, I think maybe we're having a little bit of a misunderstanding. I'm not sure we're on the same page here. I don't think you mean what you're saying."

"What?" he asked. "Must I speak slower, Mr. American? Hmmm? I want you to stick your cock in my wife Yana while I watch. Is very simple. Why so confused? I not speaking Russian, *vot pridurok.*"

Shaking Evgeni's hand off his shoulder, he turned to look back up at the second level banister. He could tell she was watching them. When she saw him, Yana quickly disappeared behind the nearest wall. *Son of a bitch*, he thought. *This is all a big joke.* He started to laugh, maybe a bit too hard. The stress was finally bursting out.

Then Evgeni started to laugh. "Why laughing? What is funny?"

"Wow, Geno. Christ, you had me going there for a moment, the both of you." He pointed up toward the second floor. "I've had some strange things said to me while on the job, some *very* strange things, but that really took me for a loop. Nice job."

"Loop? What is loop?" Evgeni asked. "I don't know what we are haha-ing about. Very serious. I want you to fuck Yana, and I watch."

"Ok, Geno, enough of this. Please stop saying that. It's not funny anymore."

Evgeni took a step closer to Hershel, and his face hardened like dry dirt. "I not funny. In fact, I rarely joke. I not comedian. I not make jokes for living. I make music. I own companies. I have more money than I know what to do with. When you laugh, it insult me. I no like that, not one bit."

Hershel's face dropped, as did his stomach. This wasn't a game. Evgeni Sokolov wasn't joking. He stared at the smaller man for a long time, completely unsure what to say. Regardless of what was folding out between them, he had to be careful with his words. "Geno, look…let's keep this relationship professional. No need to be crass."

"Crass? What crass? Look, let me make simple for you." Evgeni pulled his smart phone out from his shirt pocket and scrolled through it. "I want house, *da*? I like house very much, but it just house. I can buy house anywhere I want. I can buy another condo in New York City if I want. There are many house like this in much nicer places. Here, give me credit card."

"Excuse me?"

"Credit card, please. I don't steal money. I have much more money than you. No reason to take yours. Give."

Hershel hesitated, but eventually pulled his wallet from

his back pocket. He had no reason up to this point to not trust the man, though he could do without the constant reminder of how much less he was worth.

Evgeni took his Visa card and punched in the numbers on his phone, then handed it back to Hershel. He tapped a few more commands into the screen, then nodded. "There. You are now ten thousand dollars richer."

"Excuse me?" Hershel's heart hammered. His brain waved, and his heart told him the man was now lying to him. His phone dinged. Quickly, he checked his cell and noticed the bank notification informing him of the recent deposit. He stared at the screen with a desert dry mouth. "How..."

"And that is only little bit of what I can give you, Hershel. Obviously that amount is to keep what we discuss between three of us. To keep hush-hush. Yana and I very famous. No need to let our business become public, *da*?"

Knees weak, Hershel felt like throwing up. He couldn't take this money. Even as a charitable gift, he couldn't begin to explain to Monique how a cool 10K suddenly materialized into their joint checking account. Even if—and it wasn't even an *if* at this point, but *when*—he declined Evgeni's disgusting offer, the money would have to be given back. He didn't need the headache. He just prayed his wife hadn't gotten the same notification yet.

"Geno, I can't accept this money."

Evgeni waved him off. "Yes, you will. This is to keep mouth shut. And if you accept offer, and I believe you will, my friend, there is much more where that come from."

Much more where that come from... Hershel didn't grow up with money. The Merkley's weren't exactly poor, but they didn't have the type of income other kids wore on their shoulders and backs. He didn't envy them, only pitied them for the things they would never have to work for and appreciate. He busted his ass for everything he had. In high school, it was material things like clothes and shoes, to match his friends. As an adult he wanted to live a comfortable life and provide his wife with as much happiness as he could. They may not have been wealthy, but they weren't hurting either. He stared at the bank notification, at the shiney new deposit, and, though it pained him to even consider it, he wondered just how much more there was to be given…

Before he knew what he was doing, he ground his teeth and asked, "What do you want from me?"

He could hear Evgeni's smile. "Just like I say. My wife like you. She see you on internet. She like your picture, she like you in person. She want you to fuck her, and she want me to watch while you do it. She like that, me watching. Honestly, I did not like at first. It make me jealous. But…it make her happy. She happy, I happy, we happy. It no big deal anymore. It only have to be one time thing for you, Hershel. We do it here, now, I give you more money, we buy house, and we never speak of it again. And don't worry, my friend." He stepped closer and whispered, as if someone else in the empty house would hear. "I no touch you. I only touch myself."

A cold shiver raced down Hershel's spine. He couldn't help himself. His brain brought him to that imaginary place, where they occupied the upstairs bedroom. He saw himself huffing and dripping rivulets of hot sweat down his face as his ground his hips into Yana Sokolov. He imagined her thin, creamy body and her narrow pelvis pushing back into him, her stomach and chest a thin sheet of perspiration. There, in that room, he lasted for as long as he wanted. In that room, in his head, he could go all night. Then he saw her husband, standing at the edge of the bed, holding his prick as the two of them made Yana a satisfied woman. He heard Evgeni moan and shudder, and something spattered the sheet next to him. Suddenly Hershel was back in foyer, with Mr. Sokolov's hand placed on the small of his back.

Closing Costs

Stomach acid filled Hershel's throat as the guilt began to set in. How dare he even think of something like this as an option? Money or not, he was a happily married man. Monique Leigh Merkley brought him more happiness than any amount of hush money could. And even if—and it was a *big* fucking if—he decided to go through with it, how could he possibly live with himself? If he already felt guilty watching episodes of Game of Thrones while she was away on work assignment, how could he possibly keep something like infidelity with a supermodel a secret? He wasn't that good of a liar to begin with.

He shook Evgeni's hand off his back and took a few steps away. "I'm sorry, I can't do this."

Evgeni's eyebrows shot up. "Say again?"

"Mr. Sokolov, I'm not going to discuss this any further. I think your requests are disgusting and unprofessional, and frankly they make me sick. I believe we need to just move on with the sale of the home and forget this was even brought up."

"So now we go back to formalities, *da*? No more Geno? Ok, Mr. Merkley, we play your way. But let me say this: If you do not accept my offer, an offer I only give you one more time, then deal off. No money, no sale, *nichego*. We walk away, and you start at square one. Who else buy house where someone was murdered?"

Hershel eyed him.

"Ah, yes," the Russian continued. "You think I'm stupid? I not get this far in life by being stupid. I do research. I know why house do not sell. Young man cut father's head off in house. Why not tell me about it, hmmm? Scared to lose sale again? You should be. Say no to me again, and we leave you here with nothing. Obviously you keep money I already give you, but you get no more. Is that what you want?" Once again he placed his hand on Hershel's shoulder, and Hershel did everything he could to not break the man's tiny digits.

"You don't want that, do you? You want my money. You also make money from sale, *da*? Too much money to…how you say…piss away."

Hershel stared out the window, past the front lawn to the miles of dead cornfields beyond. He closed his eyes and let the midday sun warm his face.

"Just say yes," Evgeni said. "Make me happy. Make Yana happy. Make you happy. Surely there something you want with all that money? New car? Vacation for you and wife? Just think of it as…closing cost."

He opened his eyes, but they quickly narrowed against the light. Out past the cornfield, a figure marched up the road toward the house. Hershel nearly growled. He turned to Evgeni and gave him the 'just one moment' finger, then quickly ducked outside.

TEN

"What are you doing here, Mr. Whitecomb?" Hershel asked as his dress shoes clopped down the driveway. He stepped around the Sokolov's rental Lexus as the other man's dirty Sketchers met the blacktop. Hershel stopped him with an outstretched palm. "Stop right there."

Colin Whitecomb shrunk and threw his hands up in defense. "Hey hey, man! I'm not here to cause any trouble!" Even in his late twenties, his voice squeaked like a prepubescent teenager.

"Mr. Whitecomb, you know better than to be here. This doesn't appear to be a thousand feet away."

"But—"

"No. Now come on. Don't make me call the police again. I'm busy and don't have time for it."

"No no no! Please don't do that! I just…I just wanted to see what was going on up here." He leaned past Hershel to get a better look at the red sports car parked behind him, but Hershel stepped into his view.

Pale and sickly, the man before Hershel appeared to be a shell of kid he had seen on the news many years back. Just a teenager then, and a broken one at that, but as a grown man he still didn't seem to have the health or vibrancy someone his age should have radiated. His hair was all but gone, now just a simple brown horseshoe of thinning fluff. His white Donald Duck t-shirt draped over his malnourished form like a dirty sombrero, and his torn at the knee jeans had seen better days. Though Hershel didn't detect any track marks, he suspected the kid was using. Normal people didn't jitter like that.

"What's going on here, Mr. Whitecomb, is none of your concern." Though Hershel didn't need to intimidate the kid, he stood up straight, letting all six-foot-four tower over him.

"What? What's happening at my father's place isn't any of my concern? How dare you! I lived in that house, man. I grew up in there."

"With your brother?"

Colin Whitecomb shook, even more than before. He looked away from Hershel and scratched at his patchy stubble.

"How is Cameron these days, Colin?" Hershel asked.

The younger man grimaced. "How the hell should I know, man? Haven't seen him since..."

Something was up, and it set off vibrant alarms in Hershel's head. There was no need for Colin Whitecomb to be snooping around his father's long vacant home. Not wanting to stay too far away, Colin currently lived in a run-down trailer down the road, where he was always in arm's reach. He'd been up here before, sometimes when other realtors were busy trying to catch the white whale sale, snooping and trying to stir trouble. He once even broke in and tried to set the house on fire from the inside, which is what landed him the restraining order he was currently violating. Much like his missing brother, he had no claim to the house. It was sold to the state, and then sold to his realty company so they could do their best to fill its walls with new life.

"Why are you here, Colin?"

Whitecomb shook his head, trying his best to look nonchalant. "Nothing. Curiosity, I suppose."

"You know what they say about curiosity, right?"

"What—it killed the dog? Or cat? I don't fucking know, man! Why are you all up in my business? Quit hustling me, man!"

Hershel took a step forward, forcing Colin back. "Because I've got some very big clients in that house right now, and I am *this* close to making the sale. I'm trying to be as nice as I possibly can with you, Colin, I really am. So please don't take this personally, but would you kindly fuck off so I can get back to them?"

Tears suddenly fell down Colin's face. He put a trembling hand over his mouth. "You need to leave."

"Excuse me?"

"All of you. You ne—"

A shrill scream rang out from inside the house. Hershel whipped around as its echo lifted over the Bradford Pears in the front yard. "What the hell was that?"

"Oh, no!" Colin pushed past Hershel and dashed for the front door.

Hershel yelled, "Get back here!" and darted after him.

Colin was in through the front door before Hershel could hit the porch. The door swung back toward him, and he carefully pushed it back inward, then closed it behind him. Other than Colin Whitecomb dashing up the staircase like his ass was on fire, the foyer was completely empty. Evgeni was gone, probably going after his wife after hearing her shrill cry.

Instead of calling for Colin to come back, he yelled, "Evgeni? Where are you? Is everything ok with Yana?" He quickly checked the two side hallways, before going back to the staircase. "Mr. Sokolov? Yana?" When he heard a heavy crash upstairs, he too rushed up the staircase, two steps at a time.

By the time he reached the top, his heartbeat threatened to break his ribs. He didn't need this, not at all. He was already being weighed down with a life-altering decision, but having to drag Colin Whitecomb's scrawny white ass back out the front door didn't need to be part of it. He took a right, where both Yana and Colin had disappeared to, and slowly edged down the hallway. His fingers reached for the nearest light switch. The hall light failed to snap on above him. He flicked it a few more times with the same result.

"Colin? Where'd you run off to?" Only the slight creak of wood under his feet answered back.

"Mr. and Mrs. Sokolov? Everything ok, you two?" Still no response. Grossly, he imagined Yana and her husband getting started in the master bedroom as they waited for him to find them. He wished this was all still some sort of cruel joke, which they refused to let go, but he remembered Evgeni's money still sitting in his bank account, and that was definitely not a laughing matter. *Be a man and confront them*, he thought. In the dark, he stomped toward the end of the hallway to the open bedroom door—

—but Hershel suddenly found himself crashing sideways as something collided with his hip. His breath left him in a *whoosh* before his head made a wide, circular indentation in the drywall. Stars exploded in his eyes. He grabbed his side where someone's boot had kicked him.

Before he could react, a figure stepped out from the blackened bathroom and crouched over him. A rough hand found his throat and squeezed. Still dazed, Hershel pawed at the man's arm. He gagged as the grip tightened and pushed down toward the floor. Then a damp rag was thrust against his nose and open mouth, and just as he wondered how this was happening, a sweet, vinegary perfume lulled him to sleep.

ELEVEN

Above her head, the heart rate monitor watched over her like a personal doctor, quiet and consistent with its immediate thoughts. And when it unexpectedly decided to chatter, it startled Tara awake. The room was pitch black, even the bathroom light was turned off. She had begged Nurse Scofield to keep it on. She didn't like the dark, it scared her so bad, and she at least wanted the ability to see if her daddy was back in the room with her. The only light was her monitor as the green strobe erratically swept up and down.

Then she felt it—the reason the beeping woke her. It wasn't her legs this time. Her lower back throbbed, and the pain was so intense it made her weep. Hands curled into fists, she beat the bed, willing the pain to go away and never ever come back. But it remained steadfast, and her ECG did its best to tell her so. For a moment she couldn't find her voice, could only suck in air deeper and deeper—then it came.

The door was thrown open, and Nurse Scofield snapped the lights on. She rushed to Tara's side. "Doctor Lombardo! Quick!" she yelled. Then to Tara, "Where does it hurt? Can you tell me, sweetness?"

Tara could barely open her eyes. "My back…down here." She smack at the bed near her hip.

A large man in a white coat charged to her bedside. "Status?"

She tried to hold it back, but Tara leaned over and vomited on her blanket, the one with the piggies and cows her daddy brought for her. She started to cry again, this time out of embarrassment more than pain.

The nurse touched Tara's lower back as gently as she could. It still hurt a lot, but her touch made her feel safe.

"Could be kidney failure," the nurse said.

The doctor remained silent, then motioned for the nurse to follow him. Though they were just out of earshot, Tara could still hear them talk.

I don't know how much more we can do…
Obviously we give her more medication…
Can't. There's no more money left…
Surely there's something we can do? We can't just…
We have no choice. Just try to make her comfortable.
It's just so cruel….
You're right. But my hands are tied…

Tara did her best to stay awake, but the pain was too much. She passed out, wishing her daddy was there to hold her hand. She missed his scratchy beard kisses.

TWELVE

Hershel would have screamed. He would have fought something fierce. He would have cussed and shouted and kicked and punched with everything his forty-eight year old body could manage. If he could.

He awoke to Yana Sokolov's muffled cries. Coughing, he immediately gagged at the thick shred of cloth tied around his face. The sweet stench of chloroform still lingered in his mouth and sinuses, and he desperately wanted to rid himself of the taste. Harsh lengths of rope kept his hands bound behind his back and his ankles straight out in front of him. A few small candles were lit here and there, but a single, sixty-watt clamp light hanging from a beam in the center of the room provided the most light.

Blood was everywhere.

To his left, Evgeni Sokolov's supermodel wife was in the same shape as himself, bound and gagged, with a trickle of blood running down her nose. To her left, Colin Whitecomb mirrored them both. The scrawny man stared wide-eyed into the light. In the center of the room, a man walked a slow circle around Yana's unconscious husband, but unlike them Evgeni was not tied up. Sitting upright and legs folded, his head was down, and his arms rested on his lap. The large brown sack in the man's hands crinkled as he carefully poured a grainy white substance around the unconscious Russian. When he reached the starting point, he delicately scooped up what Hershel now recognized as salt until it completely enclosed the circle.

Something scratched the floor near Hershel.

He turned his head and found someone's hand. Only this hand wasn't attached to anyone. It was nailed to the floor and surrounded by salt.

Hershel jerked away and screamed into his gag.

The standing man turned to him. "You're awake," he said. "Good. We can start the invocation now." He dropped the bag of salt next to a large knapsack and walked toward him.

Still screaming, Hershel scooted himself away from the disembodied hand toward Yana. When she saw what made him move, she too began to yell.

"Scream all you want," the man said. "Nobody can hear you down here. Not even God."

Through his gag, Hershel shouted until his neck muscles bulged.

The man stepped closer to Hershel until he was right over him, then he knelt and looked him straight in the eyes. He shook his head. "I don't care what you have to say to me. I don't care what your name is. I don't care if you're married or if you have kids or you don't want to die. I. Don't. Care. It's not up to me what happens to you." There was no humor or vitriol in the man's voice. His words were just a matter of fact to him, spoken like a prepared speech. "This isn't about race or getting my kicks or money—at least not your money. If it were up to me, I wouldn't have chosen you. From what I could hear, you all seem like nice, decent people. You're here with me purely because of circumstance and coincidence." He angrily pointed to Colin. "You're here, you dumb shit, because you couldn't keep your fucking mouth shut."

The man looked so familiar. Hershel couldn't quite put his finger on it. He glanced back and forth from Colin and his capturer until the two became one. Though he was the same age as his twin, Cameron Whitecomb didn't appear quite has haggard as his sibling. He still had all of his hair, and his beard was much thicker. They were both quite skinny, but Cameron didn't have that sickly look his brother had adopted. He appeared healthier, sturdier, and strangely handsome for a long-missing murderer.

Closing Costs

"You can't get out of this," he continued. "So stop your fucking crying, all of you, and this will all be over quick. Hopefully your deaths will be as painless as Ishkalben can make them." He stood and faced all three of his subjects. "Honestly, I don't know what he has planned for you. Maybe you live, maybe not. I know you're all scared, even you, brother, but I cannot stress how important this is to me. I'm sorry. I truly am."

From underneath his cloth, Colin wiggled his tongue until his gag fell loose around his neck. "Please!" he cried. "Please, Cameron! I'm sorry. Please don't do this to me!"

Cameron grimaced and took a couple of long strides toward his brother. "You're sorry?" Colin cowed against the wall. "You tried to stop this! Of all people, you know what this can mean—for the both of us! Do you want her to die?"

"Please just let me go! I don't care what you do to them, just let me go, Cam!" He slowly bounced his head off the blood splattered concrete wall.

Snarling, Cameron walked back to the middle of the room. "I can't do that. I finally have what it takes to complete this invocation. If I let you go, then I wouldn't have the right amount out witnesses. Six eyes, three souls. Any less, and it's my ass. Then where would that leave her, huh? With you, you fucking junkie? Not a chance."

"I don't want to die," Colin wept.

"Neither does she." He bent over and reached into his bag, pulling out a large machete. Its black stained surface glinted in the spotlight.

Colin began to scream. He bashed his head against the wall, harder than before.

Cameron roared, "Enough!"

Hershel and the others went silent, though he couldn't control his shaking. His bladder was swollen, and his side continued to throb where he was blindsided. Luckily his head no longer hurt. He too didn't want to die. Not like this. Tied up by some freak in the basement of a house he was trying to sell. Sure, he'd had nightmares like this before. He imagined all realtors did at some point. Unfortunately, to the less fortunate, sometimes nightmares come true. He longed to call Monique, wanted to hear her voice and her reminder to wear his best suit this evening for the show. He could tell his phone was gone, as were his wallet and watch. He blinked the tears away, praying he would wake up from this mess.

Along with his blade, Cameron also carefully extracted an old leather tome from his bag. Its cover was worn, its pages torn and yellowed, and the way he grasped it told Hershel how delicate it was. "I'm going to read a few passages, and ya'll are going to repeat them when I ask you to. It's important you do this, otherwise it won't work. We only have one shot—just one—and it has to count. It would be in your best interest to do as I say. Got it?"

He stepped over to his brother, the book in his left, machete in his right. He addressed the room. "Tonight, we call upon Ishkalben, demon of resurrection, imp of revivification, and servant of the righteous one Hades, so that we may speak to one of our own. I ask of you, Ishkalben, grant us your presence, as I have done what you have requested." He turned to Colin. "Colin Whitecomb, you will bear witness to his power. Repeat after me: I bear witness, *laude erit*, Ishkalben."

Colin silently shook his head as he continued to bounce it off the wall.

Frustrated, Cameron drove his boot into his brother's stomach. Colin coughed and gagged, collapsing to his side. "Say it!"

"I…bear witness…"

"*Laude erit.*"

"*Laude…erit.*"

"Ishkalben."

"Please don't make me say it, Cam!"

Cameron held the machete out until it was inches from Colin's sweaty nose. "Ishkalben."

Colin closed his eyes, trembling. "Ishkalben."

Satisfied, Cameron then stepped over to Yana and pulled down her gag. "Now you, sweetheart. "I bear witness, *laude erit*, Ishkalben."

She immediately began screaming. "*Ty! Svin'ya amerikanskaya! A nu otpustil menya bystro! Zhen'ya, da pomogi zhe mne!*"

"Bitch, I don't care if you don't speak English or Latin. You're going to learn today." He knelt and pulled her left heel off her foot, then placed the machete blade against her toes. "You can't very well strut down a catwalk with a limp, can you? Can't imagine that would be a very pretty look. Repeat after me or I cut off your fucking toes."

Tears draining, she glanced over to Hershel, who nodded back to her. Gone were those serpentine eyes that slithered up his body only a short while ago. Pure fear had replaced her raw confidence. He felt for her.

"I bear witness," he said.

"I…bear…," she struggled.

"Witness."

"Vit—"

"Wit—witness."

"Vit…Wit—ness."

"*Laude erit*, Ishkalben."

She stared at him, confused.

He shook his head, then abruptly pressed the machete against the floor. Yana screamed as her pinky and ring toe separated from her foot. Blood squirted over the dusty concrete floor. Yana writhed against her binds, but Cameron sat his knee on her legs.

"Say the fucking words! *Laude! Erit!* Ishkalben!"

"*Laude!*" she cried.

"*Erit!* Ishkalben!"

"*Erit,* Ishkalben! *Tak bol'no!*"

Hershel wanted to puke, and he was shaking so bad that he thought his shoes might come off, but he forced himself to remain calm. If they were ever going to get out of this alive, he had to be the most composed of the three. As far as Evgeni went, he still wasn't sure if his client was alive or dead. Cameron carefully pulled the gag from his mouth, Yana's blood smearing down his cheek.

"You going to give me any trouble, old man, or am I going to have to cut something off of you too?"

Hershel glared daggers at the man. "I bear witness, *laude erit*, Ishkalben."

Cameron nodded. "Good. I like you. I hope Ishkalben spares you."

"If I make it out of whatever you're about to do," Hershel growled, "I won't spare you."

Eyeing him, Cameron turned away and focused his attention on Evgeni. He still had not moved from his sitting position. His slow, shallow breaths lifting his shoulders were the only indication he was still alive. Gently, Cameron placed his machete on the floor outside of the circle of salt, and now held his free hand high. "Lord Ishkalben, your three servants have pledged their eyes to your power. I pledge their souls to you. They are yours, if you so desire. We ask that you come forth, so that I may remunerate for your services. Ishkalben! *Veni ad me! Ostende mihi faciem tuam virtute!*"

The clamp light above their heads flickered, then dimmed, and the few candles still lit blew out. Even with his gag removed, Hershel suddenly found it difficult to breathe. The air constricted and expanded, over and over, like the room itself was gasping. Yana continued to howl in pain, while Colin attempted to melt himself into the wall.

Closing Costs

Over and over Cameron bellowed, "Ishkalben! *Veni ad me! Ostende mihi faciem tuam virtute!*"

The overhead light gradually brightened, blinding them. Inside the circle, Evgeni snapped awake and threw his arms straight up, his body going rigid. Cameron's words bloating the air, Evgeni opened his eyes, and a sound like a runaway freight train blew through his lips. A thin gray smoke poured from his mouth like liquid.

Then it stopped. Cameron went silent, as did Evgeni. The Russian's head and arms dropped, and the light above them returned to normal. The smoke continued to dribble down his chin but stopped as it reached the layer of salt surrounding it. Evgeni lifted his head.

"You beckoned?"

THIRTEEN

"I did," Cameron answered.

Hershel winced at the voice that came out of Evgeni Sokolov's mouth. Gone was the heavy Russian accent that followed he and his wife over to the States. The voice that croaked from his lips, along with the ongoing drip of gray smoke, was like nothing he had ever heard. Akin to ground-up glass in a garbage disposal. Even his eyes were different, wider and more focused, and less flippant. He looked around at the other four in the room, and seemed to admire the circle of salt enclosing him.

"I see you've once again taken the proper precautions, Cameron," he rasped.

"I've brought you what you asked for, Ishkalben. Six eyes, three souls."

The demon inside of Evgeni nodded. "So you did. You finally got something right for a change."

Cameron gritted his teeth. "I've held up my end of the bargain, demon. Now it's your turn."

Still bleeding out on the floor, Yana screamed her husband's name, but he continued to ignore her. He started to sit up, but quickly realized he had nowhere to go. "You demand nothing from me, human!" he growled. "You may have me locked away, but I still remain inside your other failures. Don't test me, or I will show you I am willing and able to break your bonds and spill your insides to feed on them. I haven't tasted man flesh for so long." The anchored hand near Hershel rapped its knuckles against the floor.

Cameron stood his ground. "And yet here you remain, bound by mere uniodized table salt. You don't get to make the commands here, demon." He shook the old leather book in his hand. "I've read this front to back. I know what I can and can't do, and what I'm allowed. I've summoned you the correct and proper way this time, and you have to do everything I demand. I've given you your fucking sacrifices. Now grant me my wish, little genie, or else I'm going to dump the rest of this bag on your head and melt you like goddamn slug!"

Hershel remained perfectly still. He'd forgotten to breathe, and when his chest began to burn, he hissed out a long, tight breath. Yana continued to wail and scream in her native tongue, and the other Whitecomb brother watched on in horror. He shook his head, as if he knew what was about to happen.

Ishkalben appeared rather unimpressed. "I know my place, little man. I did not write the invocation, I am only bound to it. You have fifteen minutes, and not a second more. You cannot touch or bring harm to the undead, or the deal is off. Personally, I hope you fuck up. I am aching to lick your bones dry."

"Are we done here, little demon?" Cameron asked.

"Just say the name."

Cameron carefully sat down in front of Evgeni and folded his legs, like a child waiting for story time. He took a deep breath and said, "I wish to speak to Harris Meade Whitecomb."

"As you wish."

Evgeni's eyes closed, and his body began to jitter like tires on a rumble strip. He inhaled deep, then let out a long sigh. His shoulders sagged, and his chin fell to his chest. Other than a soft jittering on the other end of the basement, the room went silent. Even Yana managed to hold her pain in to watch.

Then Evgeni leapt, jerking awake as if someone had struck him. He shifted where he sat, looking wildly around the room. "Who—where am I?"

"Hello, Father."

Closing Costs

Harris Whitecomb used Evgeni's neck to twist back to his son. His pupils were gone, his eyes only a dull pastel white. "What the fuck? Cameron? Is that you?"

He glared at his father. "Damn right it is."

"How…how am I here? Where am I?"

"You're back home, Dad. Don't you recognize your own home?"

Harris's eyes flashed about the room, confusion settling in his features. "I *am* home. Son of a bitch…" Then he darkened. "You little bastard. You fucking killed me!"

"Where's the money?"

The dead man's voice rose. "You little fucking piece of shit bastard!"

"Where's the money, Dad?"

"You-you-you chopped my fucking head clean off!"

"And I'd do it again in a heartbeat if it meant keeping you from beating me or molesting my brother! *Now where's the fucking money?*"

Harris ceased his rambling and stared hard at his son. He began to snicker. "I gave you everything, you spoiled little fuck. You and that prissy little bitch brother. I won the lottery for you. I bought the best house for you. I bought the best education for you—"

"And where in that did it give you the right to lay a hand on either of us? A big fucking house to hide your sickness in!" Cameron stood and paced. "You wanted to act like a bigshot after winning all that money. Wanted to go all around town flashing your sudden wealth. Money didn't change you, you Beverly Hillbilly. Even in Hell you're still the same white trash piece of garbage from Henderson, Kentucky."

Harris chuckled dryly. "I see you've grown some balls since I've been gone. Good for you. Do they cover up that hairy little pussy of yours?"

"That's what happens when you decapitate a rapist."

His chuckles turned into guffaws. He turned to Colin. "How's my favorite little bitch boy son these days? Still beating your little prick to Skinemax?"

In his dark corner, Colin pulled his knees into his chest and wept.

"You look like shit, boy. Been stickin' yourself with that goof juice, I see, just like your junkie-ass mother did. Do you miss me?"

Cameron growled, "Stop talking to him."

"Do you think of me at night when you're all by your lonesome, wishing dear old Daddy would slip under the covers with you and help you go to sleep? You might be all skin and bones now, but back then? So soft and squishy."

Colin screamed and smashed his balding head into the wall.

"Yeah, I'll bet you miss me…"

"Enough!" Cameron roared. "This is between you and me, you disgusting fuck. He's got nothing to do with this. He's only here because he forced my hand."

"I never had to force *my* hand…"

Reaching into the brown paper bag, Cameron grabbed a handful of salt and pitched it at his father. The salt grains popped and smoked as they hit him. Harris howled in pain. He turned back around and tried to lean outside of the circle, but his hands and arms immediately sizzled and blackened.

"You little shit! I'm going to—"

Cameron yelled, "What? What are you going to do? I'm in fucking charge! Me! You do as *I* say, not the other way around? Got it?"

Harris held his blistered arms against his chest, panting.

As Hershel watched on, horrified, he continued to toil towards a way out of his bonds. He worked his fingers backwards toward his wrists until he found the end of the rope. He grabbed with his pinched fingers and slowly began to

Closing Costs

pull. At first it didn't budge, and his mind worked for a better solution, but soon the rope began to slide. He sat perfectly still, making sure Cameron wasn't watching, and carefully pulled the rope from the knot, inch by inch.

"We're running out of time," Cameron continued. "All I need is for you to answer my question, and then you can go back to sucking Satan's shit-covered dick for the rest of eternity."

Harris shook Evgeni's head. "I don't have to tell you a damn thing."

Cameron sighed and then knelt down in front of his father. From his back pocket he unfolded a small photo and showed it to him. "This is your granddaughter Tara. Believe it or not, Dad, I managed to find a little bit of happiness in my life. I ran away to Tennessee for a few years, and met a sweet girl named Micha. I found love for the first time, Dad. We had a little girl, but Micha died after being hit head-on by a drunk driver when Tara was just three years old. Now... now Tara's sick." Tears sluggishly dropped down his cheeks. "She's got Leukemia, Dad. Right now my little girl is dying in a hospital bed two states away, and I have no way of paying for her treatment. Since Micha died, I don't have a dollar to my name or a pot to piss in, but I'll be damned if I'm going to let my baby die when I know how much money you had. I may be a murderer, but I'm not ignorant. I know at one time you were a living, breathing human that wasn't a complete monster. I remember back before Mom died, you seemed like a reasonable man." He stood. "Now I'm only going to ask you one more mother fucking time, and if you don't answer me, I'm going to make you very, *very* sorry. Where's. The. Money?"

Inside Evgeni Sokolov's body, Harris Whitecomb remained silent. He reached out and nodded for the photo. Cameron tossed it into the circle, careful not to disturb even a single grain. Harris lifted it with both hands and studied the photo of the granddaughter he had never seen. By the back wall, Hershel remained still, his fingers still working away at the knot.

"I can't believe it. I...I'm a grandpa," Harris said. He smiled, and something that resembled pride swept across his face.

"Dad?"

Harris's eyes narrowed, and his grin soured like spoiled milk. "I wonder if she wouldn't mind old grandpap sneaking off to her room at night, eh?" He cackled, then slowly ran his tongue over the glossy photo front.

Cameron roared, "*You son of a bitch!*"

His father continued to laugh. He bit into the top corner of the photo and tore it in half. "Once she's dead she'll be welcomed into Hell, and her grandpap will be there to keep her soft little body company."

Cameron continued to scream, his body quaking, and his fists white and ready.

Harris continued, "She'll stay with me for all of eternity, you little fuck. Not only will the demons cut and bleed her, over and over, but I'll be there to help them. I'll do things that'll make even the devil blush. That's what you get for taking my life. That's what happens when you decide to play God with me, boy. And you what the best part is, Cameron?"

His son stopped growling long enough to listen.

"There is no fucking money!"

The room went silent. Though Yana continued to whimper, Colin stopped his head bashing to listen. Blood dripped down the wall.

Cameron's shoulders sagged. "*W-what?*"

"You say you're not ignorant, but you sure think like a moron. Why do you think nothing was left to leave to your dumbfuck brother over there? I didn't win *that* goddamn

Closing Costs

much. I spent most of it on the house, a couple of cars, and horse gambling—hell, I was a VIP down at Ellis Park—and what little I had left was spent sending you two mistakes to a nice private school, but look what good that did. You two look like a young Felix and Oscar. You both make me sick. I didn't have shit left by the time you decided to split my coconut. Just enough to pay for my funeral, I suppose, if I even had one. The bank was *this* close to taking the house from us. You were too young to even know that. That realtor boy over there could probably tell you all about it. I imagine the bank owns the house now."

Eyes wide, Cameron fell to his knees as if he were shot. His head fell heavily to his hands, his world shattering. Much like the photo of his daughter, Hershel could see Cameron Whitecomb tear in two.

"Your time's almost up, boy," Harris said. "I'm done here. I'm tired of looking at your ugly faces. I'll be sure to give little Tara your love."

Fuming, Cameron punched the bloodstained floor. "Like hell it is." He stood and grabbed his book, then cracked it open and read, "*Ishkalben! Mortuus oculis meis! Daemon derelinquas nos!*"

For the first time Harris looked fearful. "What did you just do?"

"I broke Ishkalben's spell for just a little longer. He can't see us now."

"He's going to be awful pissed."

Cameron picked up his machete, and wiped his nose with the back of his hand. "Not as pissed as I am right now." He stepped toward his father.

Harris backed up until his ass was nearly touching the salt. "You can't hurt me! I'm already dead. It's against the rules!"

In a swift motion, Cameron swept away the barrier of salt with his foot. "You see, that's where you're wrong, Dad. When you're occupying a human body, you can bleed once again. And right now I'm going to do just that. I'll teach you to keep my daughter's name out of your filthy fucking mouth."

Cameron lifted the machete and swung it down. Harris went to shield his face, and the thin, stained blade sunk deep into the flesh of Evgeni's left arm. His father screamed, as did Hershel and the other two tied up on the floor. Cameron roared and took another swing, and another, until the blade broke through the bone. His severed arm flopped to the floor and sizzled at it dropped into the salt. Harris howled as his bright red blood arched over the floor in large spurts. Hershel wondered if Evgeni felt anything that was happening, or if his soul was long gone by that point. Though he wanted to hate him for putting him in a corner with his outrageous offer, he couldn't help but feel sorry for him and his wife. Beyond wanting him for Yana's fantasies, they didn't deserve this. Then again, neither did he.

At long last he felt the rope come loose on his wrists. His heart leapt for joy. He pulled his arms around and went to work on his legs.

Cameron raged as he repeatedly chopped at Evgeni's arms and chest, hoping to tear his repugnant father to pieces. He lodged the large blade into his collarbone, then continued to hack into the same spot until it opened up wider. "The devil won't even notice you!"

Suddenly Harris went ridged, and an unholy shriek erupted from his mouth. Cameron ripped the machete from the wound, and as he reached back for another swing, Evgeni's remaining arm grasped his forearm. Smoke poured from his mouth. "Naughty, naughty boy, Cameron." With the flick of his wrist, Ishkalben snapped Cameron's forearm back in a ninety-degree angle. Bones broke, and Cameron's eyes crossed, as he felt limp to the floor. The machete clattered away.

Closing Costs

Ishkalben stood, his blood now a thick tar that oozed from his wounds. His head hung sideways as the tear in his shoulder widened. "You broke the spell, worm. That's a *big* no-no. Now you die."

Hershel struggled, but once the rope finally seized through the knot, he ripped it free. He forced himself to his feet, adrenaline surging.

Ishkalben stood over Cameron and grinned as a thick blue tentacle squirmed out of his arm stump. Another one pushed out of the wide divot on this neck. Cameron held his broken arm and screamed, but his eyes flickered sideways. Before Ishkalben could turn to look, Hershel stepped forward and swung. The demon grunted as his fist connected with his chin, and he spun toward the wall. Cameron opened his mouth to speak, but Hershel swept his foot out and struck Cameron's chin. He was out cold before his head hit the ground. Even in a dire situation like this, Hershel abhorred violence. He'd only been in one serious fight in his entire life, but when those three white skinheads from high school decided he was a 'nigger' and not a man, he felt the ass beating he dished out was warranted.

Hershel picked the blood-soaked machete off the floor and proceeded to cut Yana loose. She cried in pain as he lifted her to her feet, helping her to keep the pressure off her mutilated foot. They moved toward Colin, but it may have been too late.

Ishkalben knelt over Cameron's brother, his tentacles digging deep into his pale white stomach. Somehow still awake, Colin trembled as he watched the demon pull out ropes of steaming intestines. Hershel leaned Yana against the wall and, machete in hand, stormed forward and swung. The blade sliced through the demon's neck, and with two more swings and plenty of Yana's screams, Evgeni's head rolled off his shoulders. Hershel wanted to puke, but instead he kicked the limp body aside. When his body hit the floor, Evgeni's cell phone clattered out from his shirt pocket. Hershel quickly shoved it into his pants pocket, then tried to help Colin to his feet.

"I…I can't. I think…I'm dying."

Hershel shook his head. "Not on my watch. We're going to get you out of here. Just hang on."

Pale as a ghost, Colin allowed himself to be pulled up to his feet. Right arm slung over Hershel's shoulder, his left was held firmly against his stomach, keeping what intestines that were still inside where they belonged. Gripping the machete, he held Yana up with his other arm, and the three of them shuffled toward the basement steps.

But there was nowhere to go.

FOURTEEN

Numerous bodies littered the first several steps and the floor below it, tossed into piles as if someone was in a hurry. They moaned and howled as the three approached. Though some were mostly complete bodies, many were just various severed limbs. Fingers and toes squirmed and wiggled in their direction. On the bottom step, a man's decapitated head gnashed at the air. A woman, who appeared to be an unwilling quadriplegic, rolled toward them, not heeding the light dusting of salt haphazardly thrown about the floor. When her split cranium touched the salt, her hair immediately caught fire, and after a few moments her head burst like a rotten pumpkin. Hershel stared in horror, and just as they all began to sprout tentacles, he quickly backed them away.

Colin coughed, "The elevator!" and Hershel pivoted them toward the other side of the basement. Yana hurriedly pressed the up button several times. Behind them, the mass on the stairs howled as the tentacles broke free from their fleshy binds. The stink of burning meat filled the basement—then the sound of shuffling coming their way. The elevator dinged, and Hershel carefully led them inside. Yana jabbed the door close button as Hershel leaned against the wall with Colin. A nude woman with tentacles for legs slithered around the corner and reached into the cab just as the doors closed shut.

Colin began to scream.

"Colin!" Hershel yelled. "Colin, I need you to stay calm. I know you're in a lot—"

Like a burst pipe, blood sprayed from his stomach, and a bushel of bright blue tentacles erupted from his wound. Colin howled in pain. Hershel dropped him and backed himself against the door with Yana. The tentacles swept through the cab as they continued to grow and elongate. They were quickly running out of room.

"Stay back!" Hershel yelled to Yana, putting his arm across her.

The door opened behind them, and Hershel tumbled backwards into the main level hallway, machete still in hand. Inside, Yana screamed as several of Colin's appendages wrapped around her arms and pulled her forward. Groaning, Hershel quickly sat up and dove toward the doors before they closed.

Colin's corpse, now standing, had Yana pinned upright against the corner. Thick, slithering tentacles circled her body, and one long skinny one filled her mouth. Her eyes rolled in her skull. His upper half, limp and lifeless, fell backwards, and his stomach yawned like a giant, bloody mouth. His eyes opened, and he winked at Hershel.

"She's quite the woman, wouldn't you say?"

Yana bit the blue obstruction in her mouth, and the demon inside Colin shrieked. Hershel seized the moment. He hacked at the tentacles with his blade, while Yana tore at the one filling her mouth. As soon as they broke through them, Hershel grabbed Colin's shoulders and tossed him out of the elevator cab. His body hit the linoleum floor and finally broke into two separate halves.

FIFTEEN

Yana continued to spit blood as the cab rose.

Hershel checked on her, examining her arms and stomach for wounds. A thin, mucusy slime remained on her skin. "Are you ok?" he asked.

She stared at him dumbly.

"Are you—?" He stopped. "Shit. Do you understand anything I'm saying right now? I don't know Russian. I only learned that one phrase."

She pointed to her foot. "Hurts."

He nodded. "I know it does, Yana, I understand. As soon as I can find us way out of here, I'll get you to the hospital immediately. Ok?"

"Hurts," she repeated.

"I know. But—*fuck!*" A dump truck's worth of weight suddenly dropped on his shoulders. His knees gave out, but he grabbed the handrail to steady himself. It all hit him at once. He killed a man. Maybe two, he wasn't sure. Never in his life had he seen death up close and personal. And the *thing* inside Evgeni and Colin? He wasn't a religious man, nor was his wife, but after today he might have to rethink his place in the universe. He didn't believe in demons or the afterlife. He had no reason to. He only knew what he could smell and touch, and right now his nose was full of the stink of death, and his hand still gripped the instrument used to bring it. How was he ever going to explain this to anyone? Sure, the proof was in the basement, but for how much longer?

The door dinged open, and Yana helped pull Hershel to his feet. He stood ready, waiting for anything to rush them. He held Yana back and slowly peered out.

The hallway outside of the brightly lit cab was still dark,

as he was sure the power was still cut to the switch. He held his breath and waited. Once he felt they were alone, he led her out. The door closed behind them, and the hallway immediately turned into a coffin. Luckily for them, Hershel knew his way around. He led them left, down the hallway, the machete pointing out in front of him.

"Hurts," Yana said again, this time holding her stomach.

He shushed her, wanting to keep their noise to a minimum. Once they rounded to the next hallway, avoiding all the side rooms and their closed-over doors, Hershel picked up their pace and led them into the master bedroom. He quickly closed the door and locked it behind them. Yana stumbled into the bathroom, while Hershel searched for anything big enough to barricade the door with. Unfortunately the room was kept with minimal furnishings in order to display the maximum space it offered. Virtually nothing was left from the Whitecomb days, Harris's tacky plaid and camo upholstered bedroom suit tossed out years ago. He dragged the nearest reading chair near the armoire and jammed it underneath the door handle. He doubted it would hold anyone off, but it made him feel better regardless.

In the bathroom, Yana retched into the toilet.

He crossed the floor and carefully pulled open the double glass doors to the balcony. He looked both ways before stepping out. The night was cool and breezy, an icy wind cutting through from the north. Hershel leaned over the railing to the pool deck below. He estimated there was at least a fifteen-foot drop, maybe more, with nothing to break their fall but unsympathetic concrete. He wouldn't take the chance on the pool being filled, not this time of year, even with its cover tightly pulled over. Beyond the cornfields, lights flickered in distant homes too far to hear his cries. He wished he knew what time it was, or at the very least if he was late for the banquet.

Closing Costs

He remembered Evgeni's phone.

His heart leapt as he pulled the cell from his pocket and swiped it on. He had no idea where his own cell was at, though he suspected it was still somewhere in the basement with Cameron. He struggled to remember Monique's cell number, or really anyone's number at all. Remembering nothing, he cursed himself, but it didn't really matter. He scrolled page after page in Evgeni's phone, though he couldn't understand exactly what he was looking at. His apps were in Russian, and the icons were unrecognizable. He continued searching for anything that resembled a phone app, but instead he clicked the open tabs icon.

An app already running in the background reopened. Hershel started at it blankly. He didn't comprehend exactly was it was, his eyes roaming over the various letters and numbers. Two columns separated the screen, one with a very large number containing numerous zeros, the other with the number ten thousand. His eyes were drawn to the numbers above it.

His bank account number.

Hershel's mouth went dry. It was the Sokolov's bank app, the one Evgeni used to bribe him with only hours ago. He glanced back into the empty bedroom then back to the phone.

No, he thought. *Don't you dare. You're better than that.*

His thumb reached for the off button, but his index clicked open the keyboard. He carefully tapped out several numbers and clicked the big red button on the bottom of the screen. Somewhere in the basement, he imagined his cell phone dinging.

He stepped out of the cold and back into the bedroom. "Yana? I don't think we'll be able to exit off the balcony. It's too high." When she didn't answer, he walked toward the bathroom. "Also, I have Ev—Geno's phone, but I can't read anything on it." Like the bedroom, the large, white tiled bathroom was just as dark. He flicked the light switch, but nothing happened.

The bathroom was empty.

"Yana?" he whispered. "Where are you? Is everything ok?"

He felt stupid, knowing she couldn't understand a single word he was saying, but he kept his voice low and breathy so not to startle her. What startled *him* was the inch of blood sitting in the toilet bowl. He started to tremble. His blade hand shook. Stepping past the double sink and the Jacuzzi, he forced himself toward the back walk in closet. He stared into the open door and the absence of light within.

"Yana?"

Something touched his shoulder.

Hershel yelped and spun around, ready to cut down whatever was behind him. In the dark, Yana stood there, holding her stomach.

"Hurts," she complained, tears rolling down her face.

Together, they hobbled back into the main room and sat carefully on the bed. Her face fell into her hands. Hershel awkwardly patted her back. "I'm so sorry," he said. And he was. He never wanted any of this to happen. All he wanted was to sell this god-forsaken house so his company could finally be out from under its shadow. He wanted the Sokolov's to sign on the dotted line. He wanted his seven percent commission. He wanted to dig his toes in the sand and to make love to his wife in a bungalow over the ocean. Deep down in his hands, he could still feel the ghost of the machete as it chopped into her husband's neck, and the *thunk* of his head as it rolled off his shoulders. Hershel tossed the blade onto the bed behind him, never wanting to touch the damn thing ever again.

"I'm so sorry, Yana," he cried. "I didn't want to hurt him. I… I didn't have a choice."

She sat up and wrapped her arms around his neck.

"I don't know what to do," he continued. "None of this makes any fucking sense."

He felt her lips on his neck. "Is ok," she said softly.

A shiver trickled down his spine. He closed his eyes as her tongue slid up toward his ear. Her hand swept across his chest. The room was suddenly was very warm. "What are you doing?" he whispered.

"Evgeni gone. More time for us."

For a moment he was inside of her, inside his head, pistoning in and out of Yana as she cried for him to keep going. And he did. He was strong. He was young again. Able to go for as long as he desired. Like an animal, he growled, and the slim Russian beauty under him screamed for more. In the corner by the armoire, Evgeni's headless corpse jerked himself off. Hershel seized.

Where did I stop before? He thought. *Nine, ten, eleven, twelve books…my books…our books…*

"No. Stop this right now."

Before he could even blink, Yana threw him down to the bed and straddled him. She grabbed both of his wrists and pressed them down over his head. Her grip was strong, and he could not break free. The machete handle dug into his back

"What the fuck are you doing? I told your husband—I'm a married man!"

Head back, she moaned as she ground her hips into his groin. Hershel bucked and tried to push her off, but she felt like anvil weighing him down. Letting go with one hand, she smacked him across his jaw. His ears rang, and for a moment his vision went black.

"What? You don't find me sexy, Hershel?"

When he came back into focus, he found thick gray smoke pouring from her mouth. Her voice sizzled like frying meat. "I want you so bad, old man," Ishkalben laughed. "I want to feel your middle-aged cock fill up this woman's cunt before I cut it off and eat it. How about it, Hershel? Think your wife would care?"

Hershel screamed and writhed beneath her, but she kept him pinned down with unnatural strength. The bed sheets curled around his head, muffling his hearing.

Ishkalben leaned close enough for his smoke to drift into Hershel's face. "I like you, Hershel. You show conviction. There aren't a lot of humans like you anymore."

Hershel wiggled his body and felt the machete loosen and slide sideways.

"I can help you, you know? That little…problem in the sack." The demon reached down with Yana's soft hands and squeezed Hershel's genitals. "I can fix that. Just say the word. But you must do something for me in return. Bring me more people, more souls to feed on, and I'll gladly cure you of your issues. It's a simple proposition. If I were you I'd take it. If you decline? Then I fuck you to death with his human's body." He sat up and grinned. "She wanted to fuck you so bad. She still wants to. I can hear her screams, but her passion is still there."

For a moment, the demon's grip loosened, and Hershel took advantage. He ripped his right hand free and pulled the machete the rest of the way out. Before Ishkalben could react, Hershel swung the blade. It effortlessly sliced right through Yana's cheek. The demon appeared confused. She looked down on Hershel, fingering her bloody teeth through the wide open gash.

The demon laughed. "Ahhh…I'm not pretty anymore." Then she growled, teeth snapping, and dove forward.

Hershel freed his other arm and brought the blade up between them. Yana snarled and bit the razor edge between her teeth. Her hands found his exposed neck and squeezed. Eyes wide, Hershel gagged and pushed the machete upward.

Closing Costs

The blade slipped between her teeth and pushed back until it hit the edge of her mouth. He didn't stop. Breaths coming in short bursts, he rocked the blade back and forth, forcing it deeper into her head. The demon howled, and her hands loosened. Hershel sucked in a deep breath, and in one quick motion rolled them both off the bed.

He tumbled on top of her, and his weight drove the heavy blade to the floor. Yana gagged, her severed tongue lolling. He was already on his feet and running toward the door before the top of her head rolled backwards and hit the leg of the nightstand.

SIXTEEN

There could have been demons waiting for him in every room he passed, dark shadows preparing to strike. They could have been around any corner, ready to wrap him up in their slithering octopus-like limbs. Monstrosities steeling themselves on the staircase for his decent.

He didn't care. He just wanted out.

Hershel sprinted down the hallway, his shoulders bouncing off the walls. At that point, noise be damned. Everything be damned. Though he left his weapon behind, he was prepare to fight tooth and nail to break free from those walls. Fists up, he rounded the last corner and hit the staircase, leaping down two steps at a time. His legs burned, and as he reached the bottom step, his knee gave out—

His breath left him, whooshing from his lungs as he crashed to the floor. Dazed, he tried to roll over and crawl toward the front door. Only twenty feet away, it called to him. Moonlight bled destiny across the glassy floor, lighting his way.

Beside the front door, the basement staircase was rife with action. Long blue tentacles slid over the banister, dozens of them, many bloating themselves as he watched. A strong grip seized his leg. Colin pulled him backwards, smoke billowing from his face. His lower half, now gone, was a bushel of writhing eels that propelled him forward.

"Where do you think you're going, old man?"

Hershel growled and kicked at the demon's face. Colin's nose cave inward but he crawled on. In seconds he was lying on Hershel's legs, tentacles squirming over his pants. He felt his genitals being squeezed.

"Should have taken my offer, Hershel."

Then Ishkalben screamed. Flames burst from his back, instantly filling the room with smoke. A wave of heat washed over the floor. The demon rolled over Hershel and spun, his host body now fully ignited.

A large brown paper bag dropped near Hershel's head. Above him, Cameron Whitecomb extended his one good arm, and without thinking twice, Hershel allowed himself to be pulled to his feet.

"We've got to go! Now!" Cameron yelled, his chin and cheek raw and purple.

"Were the fuck did you think I was going?" said Hershel. "Back to the basement?"

"Come on."

Hershel stopped him, grabbing the smaller man by the front of his shirt. "I'm not going anywhere with you! As far as I'm concerned, you're the reason any of this happened. My clients—the Sokolovs—are dead because of you, you little shit! I ought to kick the living shit out of you right now!"

Cameron growled back, teeth bared, "I told you I didn't have a choice! This wasn't about you, man! This was about making sure my daughter could live!" He shook his head. "I'm sorry, man. It wasn't supposed to be like this."

Without thinking, Hershel reared back and cracked Cameron across his mouth. Blood dripped down his chin. He didn't appear fazed.

"I can't live without her. She's all I got, man. Do you have any kids?"

Grimacing, Hershel shook his head.

"I do. Tara's all I got left. If I go to jail, then she's done for. I can't let that happen. Please just let me go. I have to see her."

Gradually his fist unfolded until he released his grip. He sighed. He knew deep down it wasn't the right thing to do, but had he been in the same shoes, Monique's life on the line, he would have expected the same pity. He stepped aside.

Leading the way, Cameron hurried to the front door and gripped the knob. Then he stopped.

Hershel yelled, "Open the damn door!"

Cameron shook his head, then pawed at his hair.

"Get out of the way." Hershel grabbed him by the shoulders and pulled him back, but Cameron screamed and threw his arms around Hershel, pulling him down. Hershel kept his ground. "What's wrong? Cameron, what's wrong with you?"

Falling to his knees, Cameron screamed and pulled at his hair. "Please! No no no!"

"Goddamn it, boy! What's wrong?" Hershel noticed the tentacles on the basement steps had begun to crawl their way. He gripped the doorknob, determined to leave, but Cameron pulled him backwards by his leg.

"He's got me!" he cried. Tears pouring down his face, he looked up into Hershel's eyes. "Please…help my daughter. I can't…leave…" Smoke bled between his teeth.

"I…" Hershel couldn't speak.

"Please! Tara Whitecomb…Nashville…Children's Hospital…" He released his grip from Hershel and collapsed to the floor. He screamed, his eyes bulging. "Save her!"

The top of Cameron's skull exploded. Gore splattered across Hershel's pants. His body went ridged, then fell limp, his mouth a perfect O. A long blue tentacle burst from his cranium, squealing like a newborn piglet. Hershel leapt back, away from its reach. The tentacle swept side-to-side, whipping at his feet. Cameron's flaccid body inched forward as the new appendage crept toward him. Hershel threw open the front door and took one last look before running.

SEVENTEEN

She opened her eyes and yawned. It was daytime, early morning perhaps, and though she had no idea how long she'd been asleep, she was still very tired. Carefully, she rolled on to her side to watch the sunlight peek through the curtains. She glanced over toward the reclining chair in the far corner, hoping she'd find her daddy fast asleep. Once again, he was not there. But it didn't matter. She felt good. Her legs didn't hurt, neither did her back. Though some pain still lingered, she smiled because it didn't keep her up anymore. Now she could sleep through the night, and that made her happier than Christmas morning. Behind her, beyond the door, Nurse Scofield spoke in hushed words. She couldn't hear much, just snippets of conversation.

Thank the Lord it's working…
Getting stronger…
Anonymous donation…
The goodness of strangers…

She closed her eyes, wondering if she would have hair like Nurse Scofield when she was older. She was so pretty.

EIGHTEEN

Water lapped at his bare feet as he sat on the edge of the deck. Not ten feet below him, thick patches of ruddy coral reef waved with the current. A few steps away, wooden swings posted in the sand swung with the cool April breeze. Beyond that, the sun gave in to the night, the ocean swallowing its blessed heat.

He'd never seen anything so blue. So perfect.

"Hershel?"

He turned around. The bungalow door slid open, and Monique stepped out, wearing only her two piece and a sheer white robe that flapped in the wind.

"Hey, old man," she grinned. "Are you going to stare at that sunset all night, or are you going to hop back into bed with me?"

Beaming, he continued to stare at her in silence, his heart swelling with love. Finally he said, "Be right in, Mrs. Merkley."

She blew him a kiss and closed the door behind her.

For a few more moments his eyes lingered on the fading skyline, and he relished every second he was alive. But when he realized his heart wasn't the only thing swelling, he stood with a sigh and went back inside to join his wife.

ABOUT THE AUTHOR

Wesley Southard is the author of the novel *The Betrayed*, which was named one of Brian Keene's Top 15 Books of 2017, the novella *Closing Costs*, and has had short stories appear in numerous outlets such as *Cover of Darkness Magazine*, *Eulogies II: Tales from the Cellar*, *Grindhouse*, *Dark Bits*, *Blood Reign Lit Magazine*, *The Book of Blasphemous Words*, and *Clickers Forever: A Tribute to J.F. Gonzalez*. A few of those stories are collected in his chapbook *Unfit for Burial: Four Short Stories*.

When not watching numerous hours of ice hockey, he spends his free time reading and drinking copious amounts of green soda. He is also a graduate of the Atlanta Institute of Music, and currently lives in South Central Pennsylvania with his wife and their cavalcade of animals. Visit him online at wesleysouthard.wordpress.com

Also by Wesley Southard…

THE BETRAYED

How well do you know the people around you? Your neighbors? Your coworkers? Friends? Family?

Sidney Jameson, a young single father just trying to make ends meet, is being followed. They keep to the shadows, quiet and cloaked in dirty brown robes...and they're getting closer. And what they have to tell Sidney is something terrible. Something he never knew about his past. Something he didn't want to know about his future.

The war between Heaven and Hell is the world's oldest story. Lucifer turned his back on Heaven, and God eternally cast him and his faithful to the fiery depths of Hell. Everyone knows the tale...or do we? There's only a few hours left before his twenty-fifth birthday, and with the aid of The Dark One Himself, Sidney will discover his place in the battle for humanity, and how only he can stop it once and for all.

There's only one problem. The rest of world is trying to stop him.

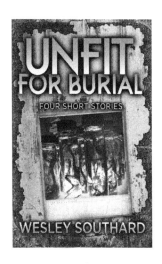

UNFIT FOR BURIAL

A man stuck on a plane of nightmares...

A woman trapped with a knife-wielding maniac...

A boy just trying to lose his virginity...

A man just trying to escape prison...

Four short stories of horror and suspense from up-and-coming author Wesley Southard.

Made in the USA
Middletown, DE
02 March 2019